The Little Raindrop
by Joanna Gray

TOP THAT

Licensed exclusively to Top That Publishing Ltd
Tide Mill Way, Woodbridge, Suffolk, IP12 1AP, UK
www.topthatpublishing.com
Copyright © 2017 Tide Mill Media
Text copyright © 2017 Joanna Gray
All rights reserved
2 4 6 8 9 7 5 3 1
Manufactured in China

ISBN 978-1-78744-216-5

A catalogue record for this book is available from the British Library

'For Nathan, Will and Karin. Thank you for inspiring me.'
Joanna Gray

One dark and stormy day, a little raindrop fell out of a cloud and flew faster and faster through the sky.

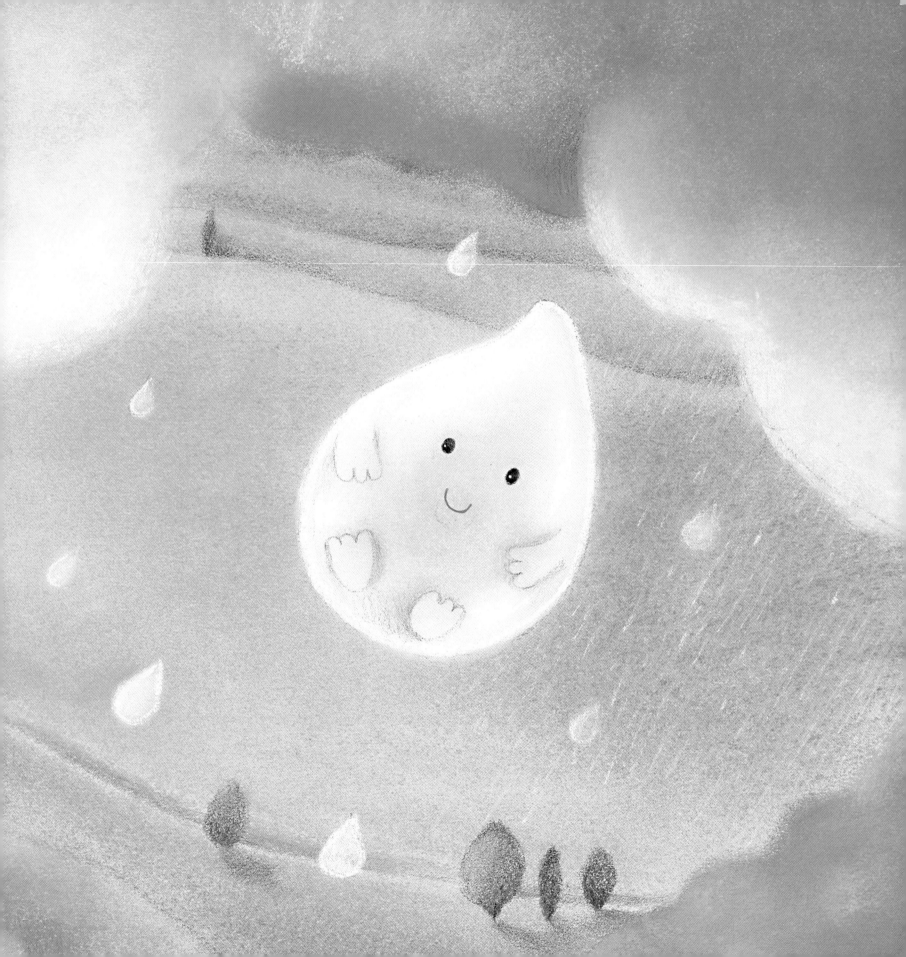

A gust of wind blew Little Raindrop sideways and
in a dazzling flash of red, orange and yellow,
he found himself inside a rainbow.

Enjoying the beautiful colours, Little Raindrop
fell through green, blue, indigo and violet before
another gust of wind blew him out of the rainbow.

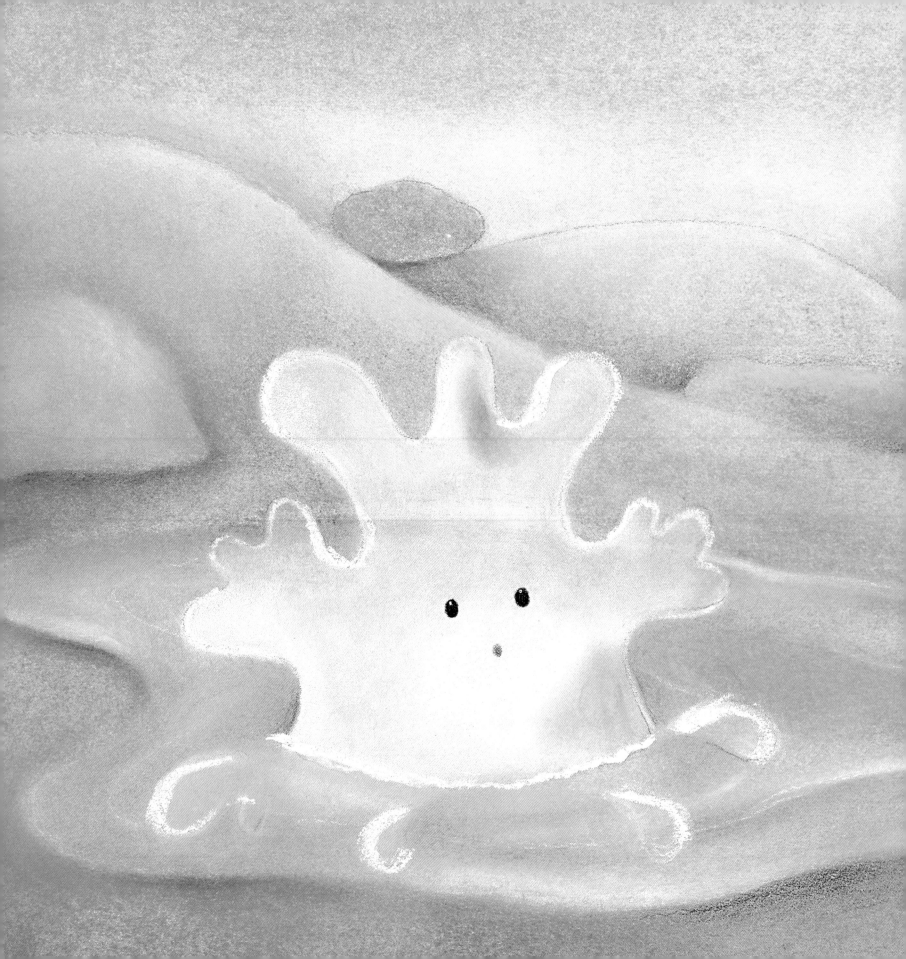

Splash! Little Raindrop landed in a shallow puddle on top of a large rock.

Splish! Splash! Splosh!
Lots of other raindrops fell all
around him, until the puddle
was overflowing.

Little Raindrop ran down
the side of the rock and
joined a stream.

In the stream, Little Raindrop
drifted through woods and bounced
over pebbles.

He played with small, shimmering fish
and watched them dart around
as deer and rabbits came to drink
at the water's edge.

Sometimes, laughing children would race sticks in the water and Little Raindrop would chase them under bridges, dodging the swirling grass and fluttering leaves.

After a while, the stream
joined a river and Little
Raindrop floated along in
the strong current.

At times, the river was calm and peaceful
and Little Raindrop watched diving
kingfishers and larger fish as they swam slowly by.

At other times, the river
was noisy and rough.
Little Raindrop raced
along rapids and dived
down waterfalls, carefully
avoiding the jagged rocks
at the bottom of the falls.

Eventually, the river reached the sea and Little Raindrop was pulled far away from the shore.

He met friendly dolphins, who played and danced in the sunlight, and listened as they whistled and clicked their greetings to each other.

One day, the tide pulled Little Raindrop back to the beach. He surfed the waves and crashed onto the shore until finally he came to rest on the soft sand.

The sun shone down on the sand
and Little Raindrop got hotter
and hotter, until the warmth
of the sun drew him up into
the air.

It was cooler in the sky and
Little Raindrop joined a cloud
that was already full of other
raindrops.

Little Raindrop was ready to fall to Earth
and begin his journey once more.